TIMOTHY and the BIG BULLY

by Jeffrey Dinardo

Simon and Schuster Books for Young Readers

Published by Simon & Schuster Inc.

New York

In memory of my grandparents
Frank & Antoinette DiNardo

SIMON AND SCHUSTER
BOOKS FOR YOUNG READERS
Simon & Schuster Building
Rockefeller Center
1230 Avenue of the Americas
New York, New York 10020

Text and illustrations copyright © 1988 by Jeffrey Dinardo
All rights reserved, including the right of reproduction
in whole or in part in any form.
SIMON AND SCHUSTER BOOKS FOR YOUNG READERS is
a trademark of Simon & Schuster Inc.
Printed and bound in the U.S.A.
10 9 8 7 6 5 4 3 2 1
Library of Congress Cataloging-in-Publication Data
Dinardo, Jeffrey.   Timothy and the big bully.
SUMMARY: With the help of his brother Martin,
Timothy learns to stand up to the class bully, Big Eddie.
[1. Bullies—Fiction.   2. Brothers—Fiction]   I. Title.
PZ7.D6115Th   1988   [E]   87-35640
ISBN 0-671-66562-6

It was time for school. Timothy finished his breakfast and said goodbye to Mama.

On his way, someone jumped out in front of him.
It was Big Eddie, the class bully.

"Hey Frog," he yelled, "you got anything good
for lunch?"
Timothy tried to run away but Big Eddie grabbed him.
"Not so fast," he said.
Big Eddie took Timothy's lunch and smiled.
"Don't tell your mom," he said, "or I'll pound you!"

At lunch time Timothy was hungry.
He saw Big Eddie eating his sandwich.

"I wish I was a giant," thought Timothy.
"Then I would show that bully!"

That night Timothy wanted to tell Mama but he told
his big brother Martin instead.
"Will you walk me to school?" asked Timothy.
"No way!" said Martin. "My friends would laugh
if they saw me walking with my baby brother!"

The next morning Timothy didn't want to get up.
He told Mama he was sick.

"You look fine," she said.
So Timothy had to get dressed.

He tried taking
the back way to school,

but Big Eddie found
him anyway.

"Nice try," said Eddie as he snatched the lunch.

After school, Martin came up to Timothy.
"Is that bully still bothering you?" he asked.
Timothy nodded.
"You should just stand up to him," said Martin.
"He's probably just a coward."
"You don't know Big Eddie," said Timothy.

The next day Timothy said school was closed,

but Mama sent him anyway.

Halfway there he met Big Eddie.
Timothy held tightly onto his lunch.

"Morning Frog," said Eddie, "Hand over the goods!"

"You are just a big bully!" Timothy yelled,
"and I am not giving you my lunch anymore!"

Big Eddie laughed.
"OK Frog," he said, "You asked for it!"

But before Big Eddie could move, someone jumped out of the bushes.

"Don't you ever bother my brother again!" Martin yelled,
"or you will have to answer to me!"
Big Eddie screamed and ran away.

"Martin!" Timothy said. "You saved me!"
"No one picks on my brother," said Martin,
"…except me."
Timothy smiled.
Then they both went off to school.

THE END

JEFFREY DINARDO grew up in New York City and in Connecticut. He graduated from Skidmore College in Saratoga Springs, New York. Mr. Dinardo has also written and illustrated another book about Timothy called *Timothy and the Night Noises.* Both of these books he says are really about himself and his big brother Rich when they were growing up. When he is not creating books, Mr. Dinardo spends his time in libraries, visiting old New England Inns and watching monster movies. He and his wife Robyn live in Mansfield, Massachusetts.